At the Café

and Other Stories

Misha Crews

Published by CWC Publishing
Because good books are essential for a happy life.

Formatting and Cover by Streetlight Graphics

ISBN: 978-0-9857167-8-3

Dear Reader,

These seven stories represent over two decades of my writing life. (And I'm pretty sure that's the scariest sentence I've ever written.)

During the time between *At the Café*, which I wrote when I was seventeen, and *Sweet Inspiration*, which I wrote when I was thirty-nine, a whole lot of life happened: marriage, jobs, schooling, our first house, my first novel. And the stories in this book are as wide-ranging as the years that spanned them. Some are romantic, a couple of them are a little bit creepy, but I'm hoping that you find all of them to be fun and entertaining.

Thanks for giving me the chance to bring you this collection of tiny tales. I hope they make you smile!

Happy Reading,

Misha

P.S. You can get in touch with me any time through my website: MishaCrews.com. I always love to hear from readers!

The Stories

At The Café

DONALD STOOD IMPATIENTLY ON THE sidewalk. Donald was usually impatient.

In front of him, cars and buses rolled by, spewing exhaust. The odor mixed with the perfume of good food and fresh flowers which wafted through the air from behind him, where urbane urbanites at the Childe Harold Café laughed and ate at round tables covered with white cloths. People walked by him – or walked *around* him, really, for the sidewalk was narrow and Donald was unyielding in his position. Half a block away, more people floated up from underground, riding the escalator out of the subway station.

It was to this group of people that Donald now directed his attention. Any moment now he expected to catch sight of a familiar figure, slim with untidy red hair, hurrying to meet him, apologizing for being late yet again: Lisa.

During the eighteen months that they had known each other, Donald had been hard-put to become tolerant of her constant lateness. But eventually he had caught on to the fact that there might be one or two facets of *his* personality that *she* would find hard to accept. And so, he had graciously acknowledged that tardiness was a part of her with which he would have to live. Then gradually he had come to realize that it was a part of her – along with other parts – that he would not be able to live without. In fact, it was her entire self that had become strenuously necessary to his survival, and he had decided, much to his surprise, that he loved her and wanted to marry her. He had said as much the last time they had spoken.

She had been surprisingly hesitant at his proposal, saying that they were both so young, that they had so much time left in front of them, why rush into things… all the things that one might expect to hear, except that Donald had *not* expected to hear them from Lisa. His Lisa. His sweet Lisa with her sweet wild-gypsy red hair and sweet wide dark eyes and sweet creamy-pale skin… But Donald halted this line of thinking firmly. It was just too mushy. And Donald was never mushy.

After their last conversation, in which Donald had proposed and Lisa put him off, he had spent several agonizing hours contemplating the prospect of a future without her as his wife. Never in his life had Donald experienced self-doubt, and he was not happy with feeling it now, just when he needed his confidence most. Then he had gotten her message to meet him here, at the Childe Harold, where they had first met. That seemed an omen, somehow: the place of their meeting, would it also be the place of their separation?

Standing on the sidewalk, Donald's impatience masked his uncertainty. What if she didn't love him? What if she said no? What would he do then?

The next second, those three questions were forgotten, pushed away forever, their answers never necessary. He didn't need a "yes" or a "no" to know that Lisa would marry him. All he needed was the sight in front of him now: Lisa running down the street, hair flying out behind her, calling his name. All he needed was the feel of her jumping into his arms, laughing. All he needed was to know that his future with her was assured.

And this he did know.

> > < <

Accidental Death

G ARY HAD FIGURED OUT A way to kill his wife and not get caught.

Funny thing was, he had known for years that he would probably end up killing her. And when he found out she was having an affair, he knew the time had finally come.

The way Gary figured it, when your wife's cheating on you there's only three things you can do: divorce her, cheat on her in revenge, or kill her. Well, he couldn't afford to divorce her. He was already cheating on her and it didn't make him feel any better. So that left only one option.

But the problem with committing murder is that it's almost impossible not to get caught, especially these days. That forensics stuff is tough to beat. And of course, the only successful murderers are the ones you never hear about.

So Gary knew he would have to be very, very smart. And fortunately, smarts had never been a problem for him.

Of course, he had suspected all along that Tina was

cheating on him. Fidelity had never played a big part in their marriage. But suspecting your wife is cheating on you and finding three empty condom wrappers in her purse while you're looking for cigarettes are two very different things. *Three*, for God's sake.

He knew right away who the guy was: Mike, that mechanic from their garage. Gary should have guessed sooner; Tina had been "having her oil changed" with an unusual frequency.

At first Gary had wanted to do something obvious like disabling the brakes on Tina's car. But his instinct for self-preservation had overridden his desire for ironic punishment, so the whole "she who cheats by the car shall die by the car" concept was out.

The really frustrating part was that there are just so many good ways to kill someone. Shooting, stabbing, bludgeoning, poisoning – all tried and true methods of removing an undesirable presence from this earth. The temptation to just shoot her in the back of the head while she was sitting in front of that vanity mirror of hers was almost too much to resist.

But there again he stopped himself. He wanted Tina dead, but no way was he going to spend the rest of his natural life in prison. He had to be careful, take his time, be smart. So, he let time go by. He put murder on the back burner, so to speak. After all, it wasn't like he was on a deadline, or anything. He waited, and he watched, and he thought about it.

In his imagination he killed Tina a dozen different

times in a dozen different ways, which was actually kind of fun. The long, steep road with the sharp precipice that ran behind their house often played some part in his daydreams. He saw her plunging off the road, eyes wide with terror, car erupting in flames as it crashed to the rocky hillside below. But tempting as these visions were, they were far too impractical, too easy for the police to figure out. He had to come up with something smarter.

And finally, one day he did.

Well, to be fair, Tina practically came up with the idea for him. She had been whining at him for ages to get a water bed. Said it would be good for her back. Gary had always resisted the idea.

"Oh sure, a water bed" he'd say. "Then I'll get a van with a painting of some chick riding a leopard. Maybe she'll have flashing red light bulbs for nipples. How does that sound?"

She always ignored his sarcasm – or maybe she was just too stupid to understand it. Either way, she kept asking and he kept saying no.

And then, about two months after Gary had found those condom wrappers in her purse, the two of them were out shopping for a new living room sofa. In the showroom, Tina dropped her keys. She reached down to get it, and couldn't get back up again. She had actually thrown out her back.

The pain was obviously so excruciating that Gary felt sorry enough for her to buy her that water bed. What the heck, they were in the furniture store already, weren't they? Tina took a couple tranquilizers and settled into the car to wait while Gary finalized the details.

The idea came to him as the salesman was showing him how the thing worked. The bed was filled with warm water. It stayed warm because the bed was plugged in to the wall. At that moment, it was as if the salesman had plugged in Gary's brain, and two red nipple light bulbs started flashing in his head.

The idea was good. He rolled it around in his mind like wine on the tongue. Yes, it was very, very good. It would bear further thinking, of course. He would have to examine it and look for holes, make sure that the cops couldn't get enough on him to send him away. But he had a feeling that this idea was the one.

He signed the receipt with a flourish. He felt almost euphoric. In the car, he magnanimously offered to call Tina's doctor to get her a prescription for painkillers. She thanked him but said she'd done it already, and that the prescription would be delivered later this afternoon.

That night, he lay on his back in bed while Tina breathed heavily in a drugged sleep beside him. His plan reeled out before him, like a movie in the darkness.

Today was Saturday. The bed would be delivered on Monday morning. The delivery guys would take down the old bed and set up the new. It would take a few hours to heat up, of course, but it should be ready by the time Tina went to bed.

Gary would graciously offer to sleep in the guest room, so that she could have the whole bed to herself for her recuperation. He would turn on her bedside radio, tune it to the classical station and turn the volume so that it played softly. She found this very soothing when she was in pain.

After he kissed her good night, she would take a couple of the painkillers, and within a half hour she would be nearly unconscious. With those knock-out pills she could sleep through anything.

Before he retired for the evening, he would turn on the hall light outside the bedroom. When he flipped the switch a fuse would blow, taking with it the hall light, the bedside radio, and, of course, the water bed heater.

From where he was standing, it would appear the hallway bulb had blown out. He would resolve to replace it tomorrow. Then he would go to bed. And in the other room, the water in the water bed would slowly start to cool, taking Tina's body temperature down with it. She wouldn't wake up. Ever.

Tuesday morning he would get up, shower, and get dressed. He would peek in on her, assume she was sound asleep, and close the door softly, not wanting to wake her.

He would get in his car and drive to work. Sometime around two o'clock, the cleaning woman would arrive and make a gruesome discovery.

He couldn't be sure exactly what time Tina would die, but the point was that she would be dead. When the police interviewed him they would tell him about the blown fuse. He would appear to put the pieces together and break down, crying "*Oh my God, I killed my wife!*"

Truer words could not have been spoken.

Gary grinned into the darkness. He had it. He really had it.

Well, there was no way he was going to sleep tonight. He was just too excited. He got up and dressed silently. He would go out for a quick drink. Maybe tomorrow morning he would bring Tina breakfast in bed. Seemed like a nice thing to do.

The garage door opened in front of him, revealing a desert sky full of stars. The moon shone brightly, almost benevolently. This time next week, he'd be a free man. He couldn't believe his luck. He pulled out of the driveway and started down the hill.

No, he corrected himself. It wasn't luck. It was smarts. He'd always had them.

The car picked up speed. He put his foot on the brake, but nothing happened. He tried again, and still nothing. He reached for the emergency brake.

But he was too late.

In the bushes by the side of the road, two people huddled in the shadows, watching the flames rise against the night sky.

"I told you it would work," Mike said.

Tina sighed. "I know. I just feel guilty. He was so nice today when he thought I'd hurt myself...buying that bed and all."

Mike rubbed her shoulder. "Look, the man was a pig. He thought you were unconscious from pain pills and he was driving out to see his mistress."

She sighed again. "You're right. But...are you sure the police won't suspect us?"

"Trust me. I know how to fix cars." He looked down at the wreck burning in the valley. "They'll say it was an accidental death."

> > < <

Murder, Sweet Murder

T HERE WAS A BODY ON the floor.
Casey blinked and looked around the empty coffee shop, then blinked again and looked back down. No, she hadn't imagined it.

There was a body. On the floor. Of the shop.

God, this morning was going all wrong.

She reached for the phone on the wall, and her fingers found the buttons: 9-1-1. Her voice was calm, but her hand shook a little as she gave the officer the pertinent information. He asked her to stay on the line until the police arrived at the scene, but she ignored that request and hung up.

A thought hit her at the same instant the receiver hit the cradle. *Fingerprints.* She shouldn't have touched the phone, should she? The shop was a crime scene now, and at a crime scene you weren't supposed to touch anything. Anybody who watched as much *Law & Order* as she did should have known better.

That morning her alarm hadn't gone off, and she had woken up abruptly a mere ten minutes before she had to leave the house. The worst part of that was that she had been dreaming that she was already awake, and that she had gotten up early and made herself blueberry pancakes. She could still taste them as she stood under the hot shower, washing the sleep out of her eyes.

The taste had been so compelling that she decided she had to find a way to make her dream a reality. She only lived five minutes from the shop. She would dash over, open up and take care of the five a.m. crowd. Rose would arrive at six to help out. When things finally slowed down, Casey would steal away, drive home and have the breakfast she was craving. She would even make extra to bribe Rose with, if necessary.

But no such luck. If only she had bought that new alarm clock last week, the way she'd planned. The guy on the floor would still be dead, of course, but at least she would have had those blueberry pancakes.

Okay, that was harsh. And selfish. She shouldn't be thinking of food at a time like this. She should be waiting outside for the police, with an appropriately subdued air of sadness at the loss of human life.

The cowbell that hung over the front door clanged. Casey looked up and felt relief flooding through her at the sight of the navy blue police uniform.

"Hi Jeff," she said, as if this were just a day like any other.

"Hey, Casey," Jeff said. "What've we got here?"

She gestured towards the thing on the floor. "It's Hindeman."

"*Frank* Hindeman?" Jeff took a few steps to the

left so he could get a better view. He let out a low whistle. "We'll have to put the whole county on the list of suspects."

He touched the two-way radio that was clipped to his coat, and spoke some official-sounding words. Casey didn't bother to try to understand them.

"We'll have a few more cars here in a minute, and the Coroner's office is sending a wagon." He put a finger under her chin and lifted her face. "You with me, Casey Walker?"

Casey blinked. No, to be honest she wasn't anywhere *near* with him.

"Yes," she said.

"The only business you'll be getting in here today is us cops," he said. "So I hope you laid in a goodly supply of donuts. Do I smell fresh coffee?"

Casey nodded. "I turned on the machine first thing when I came in, just like always," she said.

"Where is it?"

She pointed.

"Okay," he said. "Since you already touched it I'm making an official decision that you should keep it running. And have a cup yourself, why don't you. You look a bit green around the gills."

She took Jeff's advice and had a cup of coffee and a muffin. Blueberry. Then she sat at the corner table and watched as the shop filled with people.

Cops. They looked at everything. Around everything. Under everything. They asked her questions.

What time did you get here? What time did you leave yesterday? Did you notice anything strange when you arrived this morning?

Strange? Why yes, she wanted to say. *It was the darnedest thing. I walked in and there was a dead person on the floor.*

At six o'clock on the dot, the bell rang and Rose walked in.

Just like with Jeff, Casey felt an almost ridiculous sense of relief at seeing her. Rose, with her hand-knitted sweaters and corduroy pants and soft gray hair, was the kind of person you wanted with you at a time like this. She was the kind of person who could just make everything all right.

"One of the officers outside told me what happened," Rose said. "How awful. You found him?"

Casey nodded.

"I'm so sorry, my dear," Rose said. "That must have been terrible for you. Can I do anything?"

"No, thank you," Casey said. She took Rose's hand. "I'm just awfully glad you're here."

They watched as the body was carted out. Jeff disconnected himself from a cluster of uniforms and crossed the room to sit down with them.

"Whew! What a mess," he said.

"How was he killed?" Rose asked.

"Screwdriver to the heart," Jeff said. "Probably a quick death, not that he deserved it that way."

"Do they know what happened?" Casey asked.

"Doesn't look premeditated. They think he got in an argument with somebody and the killer just grabbed the first thing he could." He looked at Casey. "You keep a screwdriver under the counter, by any chance?"

She nodded absently. "It's for that cash register. Darn thing's always jamming up. But Jeff, why do you think Frank was *here*, of all places?"

"Well hell, Casey, everybody in town knows you close at two in the p.m. And most folks probably know that the lock on your back door is acting up. And everybody knows that you and Hindeman had words the other day."

He looked at her. Suddenly his gaze was sharp, penetrating and very official. "Didn't you?"

Casey looked back with a coolness that she did not feel. "If you want to have *that* discussion," she said, "you'll have to wait until my attorney gets here."

Jeff looked hurt. "I was just making conversation," he said. "No need to get testy."

As he walked away, Casey let out a deep breath. "Good thing I moved here from the city," she said, "to get away from all the violence."

Rose patted her hand. "Don't worry about him. He'd never arrest you without proper evidence."

It was nearly noon when the last officer left. Casey locked the front door with a feeling of relief. At least that was over.

She turned to find Rose staring at the bloodstain on the floor.

"Not very appetizing, is it?" Casey said. "I doubt the customers will like it much."

"There are people who specialize in cleaning this sort of thing," Rose answered briskly. "I'll make some calls this afternoon."

Casey started collecting the cups and coffee stirrers that littered the tables. "Hindemen really was a bastard, wasn't he?"

"He was the only truly evil person that I ever met," Rose said. "Evil to his very soul. We grew up together, did you know that?"

"I had no idea."

"We were inseparable as children. When we were only seven years old he told me he had fallen in love with me, and that he wanted me to marry him and come live at his house. Of course I said no, that I would never leave my mother and father. So do you know what he did? He told people that my father had – well, *touched* him. Inappropriately." Rose gave a delicate cough.

"It wasn't true, of course, but that didn't matter. Rumors spread, and the stress of it gave my father a heart attack and he died. My mother followed a year later."

Casey couldn't believe what she was hearing. "Rose, did you –"

"For years I prayed for the strength to forgive him, even as I watched him destroy one life after another. And then, last week when I saw how he spoke to you, how he threatened to tell everyone about what

24

happened to you before you moved here, I knew that God didn't want me to forgive him. God wanted me to send him to hell, where he belongs. And so I did. It was really very easy. And...sweet."

She smiled with satisfaction. "You know, dear, neither of us has eaten all day. You must be famished. Why don't you come home with me and I'll fix you something to eat. It's the strangest thing, but I have a terrible craving for blueberry pancakes."

> > < <

The Pleasure Of Refusing

SHE HAD SEEN HIM MANY times before, as she walked her dog around the apartment complex. He came mainly on Sundays, to accompany his parents to church. Sometimes he would arrive on Saturday evenings and stay the night.

He never spoke to her, except an occasional "Hello" as they passed on the walk. He would shy away from the prying beagle nose of her dog Argyle, although she knew that he did not have an aversion to dogs; she sometimes saw him walking his parents' boxer, which, in her opinion, was much nosier than little Argyle. He was also friendly with the dogs of many other neighbors. So it must be that he disliked her dog in particular – or perhaps it was just her.

Of course, why should he like her? In all honesty, as she stood before the mirror she knew that there was nothing much of interest staring back at her. But would he try to look beyond the outward appearance, see if there was someone amusing, someone kindhearted, someone attractive lurking underneath? No. Men like him never did. She was almost used to that by now.

Still, it hurt. And still, she liked him.

Of course, why shouldn't she like him? His face was open and friendly, and he had a laugh that warmed the heart. She wondered if he would laugh at her jokes.

That night in the rain, she almost ignored him. Almost walked by with her head down, ignoring him so he wouldn't have the opportunity to ignore her first. It was a Saturday, so it wasn't surprising to see him there, as she took Argyle on his last walk of the day. What *was* surprising was that he seemed to be arguing with the driver of a taxi which was stopped in front of the building. She had never heard him argue.

At first she avoided the impulse to linger and listen, although she did hear enough to realize that the dispute seemed to be about the about the fare the driver had charged. But by the time she had circled the block he was still there, still searching his pockets frantically, still arguing.

And then it all became clear. A wallet lay on the ground, almost under the taxi. It must have fallen out of his pocket when he stepped out of the cab, and now he couldn't find it. Without a word she stopped beside him, bent down and picked it up. As she straightened up and handed it to him, she met his eyes through her rain-spotted glasses. It was the first time he had ever really looked at her, she realized. And a second later she realized something else, as well: he was drunk.

Argyle stared up at her reproachfully as he shivered in the downpour. Water from the man's nose dripped into the wallet as he opened it to remove some bills. Why was she still standing there?

As the cab driver took the money, he looked at her and said, "Lady, you'd better get your friend to bed. He's completely smashed."

The cabbie seemed to know what he was talking about, she reflected, watching the taillights disappear into the night. Then she turned to her new charge. What did one do with a drunken man?

He started to sway, and instinctively she put out her arms to steady him. Then she sighed. If she had to do it, she had to do it.

She helped him into the building and into the elevator. He leaned against the wall and she was tempted to leave him there – just walk out and let him wake up the next morning stretched out on the elevator floor.

Instead, they made a brief stop in her own apartment, so she could drop off Argyle and rid herself of her soaking raincoat.

They made it up to his parents' apartment without incident. She knocked and got no answer. They must be in bed already.

"I'll need your keys," she said, speaking for the first time.

He tried to reach into his coat to get them, but he seemed to have forgotten exactly how a hand fit into a pocket. Finally, she became impatient and did it for him – first the left coat pocket, then the right. No keys.

No keys?

Wait – the pants. She propped him up against the wall, opened his coat, and got the keys from his left front pocket.

As the door swung open, the boxer came darting out of the darkness, charging straight for them. She almost dropped her charge and ran, but the dog stopped at the last minute, sniffing the air, then wagged his tail.

All right.

She took a deep breath, then guided her charge into the apartment. The kitchen light was on, and she could see the living room sketched in lines of charcoal gray.

"Couch," he mumbled, and she took him over to it, gently helping him to sit down. She straightened up and gazed down at him, slumped there in his soaking wet clothes.

No, she couldn't leave him like this.

She pulled him back on his feet and, holding him with one hand so he wouldn't fall over, stripped off his raincoat and suit jacket. She removed his tie. Then she tossed them over a chair and examined the rest of him. The bottoms of his trousers were wet. Well, that was too bad. She was not talking off his pants.

She gave him a little push on the chest and let him fall back onto the couch. Then she knelt and removed his shoes and socks. Immediately, he swung his legs up onto the couch and lay down. She found an afghan on the back of a chair and covered him with it.

She left his keys on the chair and got back to her own apartment as fast as she could.

The next day was bright and clear, with a high, arching blue sky. It was late in the morning when she saw him, coming home from church with his parents. Argyle tugged impatiently on his leash and she began to oblige, walking faster. But then she saw that the parents were going inside, and the son was not. He was looking at her.

The first thing she noticed when they came face to face was that his eyes weren't even red. He looked as if he had never taken a drink in his life.

He smiled his open, friendly smile. His eyes were as blue as the sky.

"I owe you a thanks," he said. "I don't know what I would have done if you hadn't helped me out last night."

"Don't mention it."

He smiled again. "It was beyond the duties of a neighbor, and I really appreciate it."

She smiled back but did not reply.

Discomfort passed briefly – oh so briefly – over his face, then the smile reappeared as he thought of something that would make everything right. "I thought that maybe, if you don't mind, we could have dinner sometime."

She didn't answer right away, and he looked at her strangely, as if she looked different. Well, that was fine. She felt different.

"No." Her voice was polite but firm. "But thank you all the same."

He was surprised. "Are you sure? I mean –"

"Yes, I'm quite sure."

He walked away, and she watched him go. He was shaking his head.

Then she turned and started off in the other direction. She felt good. Admittedly, there had been few times in her life when she had the pleasure of accepting an invitation from someone so handsome. But never before had she had the pleasure of refusing.

> > < <

My Funny Valentine

"THAT'S IT?" RONALD STARED AT the dusty box of chocolate. "That's all you have left?"

The girl behind the counter shrugged and looked bored. "It's because of the snow. Streets are blocked, trucks can't get here. We shouldn't even be open today." Her eyes took on an accusing light, as if Ronald's mad dash through the store in search of a last-minute gift were the only reason her manager was keeping the place open.

Ronald frowned. This was all wrong. It was Valentine's Day, and he needed to get a gift for Susie. Chocolates weren't exactly the best thing for a sick person, but she'd had the flu for a week and she deserved something to pick up her spirits. Besides, in some ways it was his fault that she was sick in the first place.

"How much?" he asked.

The clerk sighed, turned the box over and rubbed some dust off the price tag. "Twelve dollars," she said.

He took another look at the box. He'd found it way at the back of the shelf, behind some cans of cat food. One corner had a very slight dent in it. "Are you sure it's still, you know, good?"

Another bored shrug. What did she care? "It says the expiration date is 2016, so yeah, it's probably still okay."

Ronald sighed and counted the money onto the counter. She pressed some keys on the register and handed him a few cents in change. "Do you have a paper towel or something?" he asked her, eyeing the dust on the box with disdain. He couldn't give the thing to Susie looking like that.

The clerk fished under her counter and came up with a couple of old napkins which she handed over reluctantly. Ronald grabbed the box and the napkins and walked out into the cold.

He shivered automatically, hunching his shoulders as he made his way down the street. At least the snow had stopped, although the sky promised more flakes were on their way. He stopped at the trashcan on the corner and cleaned the box as best he could, tossing the now-gray napkins into the can before continuing on his way.

The weather had lousy timing: February 12, and the county gets hit with its worst snowstorm in twenty years. Supply trucks couldn't get into town, so stores were stuck with what they had. The drugstore was completely out of Valentine's Day cards, none of the florists had any flowers left at all, never mind roses. He had been trying for hours to find something – anything – to get for Susie. This was an important day, maybe the most important day in his life since he'd become a man.

Today was the day he was going to ask his best friend out on a date.

Ronald and Susie had known each other since they were kids. They'd met on the first day of Kindergarten. At arts and crafts time, he was the only kid in class without his own pair of scissors, and he'd been too shy to tell the teacher. Susie had seen his troubles and had slid her scissors over to him without a word. They'd been best friends ever since. It was only recently he'd realized maybe being friends with her wasn't enough.

He could still remember the funny little braids she'd worn that first day, and the way her freckles made her nose look like it had been sprinkled with cinnamon sugar. Even at the time he knew it was a funny thing for a six-year-old boy to think, but everything about Susie had made him feel a little strange. Now here they were, years later, and he was looking at her in a whole new way. Strange again, but wonderful-strange.

Two weeks ago they had been playing basketball. Stupid to play b-ball in the cold like that, but they'd both needed to get outside for a little while. He'd gone in for a dunk, trying to show off a little, and she'd blocked him – probably a little better than she'd meant to. They'd fallen to the blacktop together, all tangled up and laughing. Their faces were close together. Her lips were very red from the cold, and he suddenly knew that he wanted to kiss them. Wanted to kiss her – and more than once, too.

He'd completely chickened out. It embarrassed him to think about it now, but he'd jumped up before she could see the wanting in his face. He had helped her to her feet and tossed her the ball. They'd finished their game as the sky had started to turn dark. The very next day she'd had a sniffle, which turned into a cold which turned into the flu. He'd wanted to ask her to go out with him *on* Valentine's Day, but that was now out of the question.

But there was something he could still do: on Valentine's Day, ask her out.

He smiled to himself. His English teacher would appreciate the way he'd worked that out.

He felt pretty sure she'd say yes. But as he rounded the last corner and walked up the front steps of Susie's house, Ronald's nerve started to fail. What if she said no? What if she didn't want to go out with him? He looked at the box of chocolate in his hand, red and shiny in the gray winter light. Little bits of dust were still sticking to the plastic shrink-wrapped around it. He'd thought it was a romantic gesture, but what if Susie just laughed when she saw it?

To be on the safe side, he stuck the box in his jacket and zipped it up tight. He'd see what kind of mood she was in first, then, if things seemed right, he'd pull the chocolates out and surprise her.

He rang the bell and waited, rubbing his hands together. Man, it was cold. He couldn't wait for spring. Ronald thought about things that he and Susie could do together in the spring: taking in baseball games… maybe necking under the bleachers…. His face got red at the thought, and when the door opened he jumped.

"Susie!" His voice seemed too loud. "You look great."

"I look like hell," she said stuffily. And she did, but to him she also looked wonderful. She always looked wonderful to him, and that was the truth. Why had it taken him so long to realize it?

She tightened the belt on her robe. She was wearing slippers and her nose was red. "Come on in," she said. "My temperature's down today; I'm probably not contagious."

"Probably?" he struggled to keep his voice normal as he stepped inside and closed the door. "Does that mean there's a chance that I might catch the same creeping crud that you've got?"

"Small chance." She walked into the living room and plopped down on the couch. Blankets and pillows were arranged in a messy, comfortable-looking pile. Looked like she'd been camping out there for a while. A small waste basket overflowed with tissues. "Are you man enough to risk it, or do you want to take off?"

"I don't know." He nudged the trash can with his foot, and one fluffy white tissue fell off and dropped softly to the floor. "This place looks like a medical waste disposal station."

"Oh hush." Susie pulled her legs up under her and grabbed the remote. "I'm watching *Ren and Stimpy*. Take your coat off and stay awhile."

"*Ren and Stimpy*? Cool. Very retro." He sat down in an armchair, ignoring her invitation to take off his coat. He had something to ask her first.

"You want some orange juice or anything? We've got chicken soup. Lots and lots of chicken soup."

"I'll pass for now, but thanks anyway."

"Suit yourself." She raised her hand to un-mute the television.

"Wait. Suze –" He broke off, suddenly too nervous to continue.

She lowered her hand and looked at him. Her eyes were wide and completely incurious. "What?"

This was the moment, right? This was the time to say it: *I really like you. Be my Valentine?*

He took a deep breath and started to unzip his jacket.

"Ronnie!" Susie's mom came around the corner.

"Oh, hey Mrs. Berkley," he said weakly. Up went the zipper again.

"So you came to visit our sick little girl? And in all this terrible weather? That's so sweet."

"Mom." Susie rolled her eyes. "Come on, enough with the Donna Martin stuff, okay?"

"You're thinking of Donna Reed, dear." Mrs. Berkley patted her cheek and headed toward the kitchen. She stopped at the door and turned around. "Ronnie, I don't think I've seen you since your Bar Mitzvah. How have you been? How are your parents?"

"Just fine, Mrs. Berkley, thanks."

"Well tell your mother I said hello."

"I sure will." His voice cracked on the last word, and he pressed his lips together self-consciously.

Mrs. Berkley gave him a knowing smile as she finished her exit from the room. "If you need me, just holler," she called.

Susie shook her head. "She gets weirder all the time."

Ronald shrugged and gave a half-smile. He wasn't in the mood to discuss the bizarre behavior of parents, hers or his. He was almost fourteen years old now and he was here to ask the girl he liked best to be his Valentine.

He took a deep breath, unzipped his coat and pulled out the chocolates. "Susie," he said, "these are for you."

Slowly, very slowly, she reached out and took the box from his extended hand. She turned it over once, then again. The room echoed with silence.

Then Susie looked up at him. And she smiled.

> > < <

The Bell Tower Man

M ARY STOFFEL WAS HALFWAY TO school when she realized that the school bell hadn't rung. This was so strange that Mary stopped and stood right still, listening with both ears.

She heard the wind rustling through the tree leaves above her head...the brook chuckling along to her right...and the crunch of a tiny foot on a tiny twig behind her.

She whirled around, hands on hips. "Adeline Stoffel, go home this instant!"

There was nothing in front of her but the trees, and the wind and the brook were all that answered. Nevertheless, Mary narrowed her eyes and spoke again. "Da said you're not to be following me to school anymore! Now get along home!"

She waited the length of three heartbeats, then turned and continued up the path.

As expected, the sound of tiny pounding feet rushed up behind her and short, fat arms grabbed her around the waist. Mary fell to the ground, laughing. She tickled her sister until they were both breathless with giggling.

Then Mary remembered herself and stood up, pulling Adeline along with her. She picked leaves out of her sister's hair with a fury.

"You're such a naughty one, little sister! What do you think Ma and Da will do when they realize you've run off? Worry themselves to death, most likely."

She took Adeline's chin in her hand and looked down at her. "Now go home, and let me get on my way to school!"

"But the bell hasn't rung!" Adeline said. Her blue eyes were wide with happiness. "So it must be Saturday, and that means no school!"

"It's not Saturday, it's Thursday. And Miss Hobbes is late, that's all." Mary sighed, then grabbed Adeline's hand and continued up the path towards the schoolhouse.

Adeline, floating on winged happiness at being taken along, felt brave enough to say, "Maybe she ran away, and you'll never have to go to school again!"

"Or maybe she climbed a tree and married a monkey!" Mary said.

"Maybe she was taken by the Bell Tower Man!"

Mary tripped, then recovered her balance and went on as if she had never missed a step. "There is no Bell Tower Man," she said firmly. "You're too big of a girl to believe in stories like that."

"It's not a story!" Adeline protested earnestly. "It's a real live ghost! Christian Aart saw it. He told me so himself."

"Christian Aart likes the sound of his own voice better than he likes the truth, and you'd be wise to remember it!"

They came out of the woods into the clearing near the schoolhouse. The doors were closed, the curtains inside were drawn. A few boys were playing leapfrog on the grass.

"Hi! Mary!" Zachariah waved. "Miss Hobbes isn't here!"

"We didn't hear the bell ring!" Adeline chirped importantly.

"That's because there was no one here to ring it," said Christian. "Miss Hobbes…has disappeared."

Mary looked at him crossly. Christian was the only boy in school who was taller than she, and he thought that made him superior to her.

"She's just late," said Mary.

"She's *never* late!" Zachariah and Alberick cried together.

"Something's happened," said Christian knowingly. "Has anyone noticed anything odd going on lately?"

"Barent the Gatekeeper," said Alberick. "I think he's up to something."

"What makes you say so?" Mary asked curiously.

"His hair is red. And his face is always as red as his hair."

"What nonsense!"

Christian scoffed at her. "If you're so smart, why

don't you tell us where Miss Hobbs is?"

Before Mary could think what to say, Adeline piped up with confidence. "We think it was the Bell Tower Man!"

"Of course!" said Christian. "It's the only thing that makes sense!" He jumped up on a tree stump and raised his arms. "We must go at once to the Bell Tower and rescue our poor teacher! Who's with me?"

"I am!" said Alberick.

"And me!" cried Zachariah.

Mary opened her mouth to protest when Adeline cried out enthusiastically, "Us too!"

Then she looked at her big sister. "Right?" she asked hopefully.

Mary sighed.

The bell tower was taller than Mary had remembered. The stairs inside curved upwards into darkness.

"Are you sure you want to do this?" Mary asked her sister.

"Um...uh-huh." Adeline said.

"All right," Mary said.

She stepped inside and started climbing, with Adeline close on her heels. Christian, eager for this adventure though he had been, did not protest when Mary took the lead.

"I'll bring up the rear," he said. "So nothing sneaks up on us."

They giggled and shuffled their way up the stairs until Mary's hand, outstretched in the dark, touched the trapdoor to the bell loft. Her heart beat faster.

She looked down, trying to see her sister. Adeline's eyes glowed through the darkness, alight with fear and excitement.

Christian tapped Mary's leg. She kicked at him out of habit. "Well, go on!" he said.

Right. Mary squared her shoulders and reached upward. She grasped the handle firmly and pushed.

Up it swung, lighter than she had expected and almost completely silent. She raised her head and peered around, blinking. Light spilled into the center of the loft from the open archways on each side, but puddles of pitch dark filled the corners in between. A tug on her skirt, and Christian's imperious voice floated up from below.

"What do you see?" he whispered loudly.

"There's nothing up here," Mary whispered back. "We should go."

She started to close the trap, but murmured cries of protest stopped her.

"Hold on, hold on!" That was Zachariah.

"We want to see!" That was Alberick.

"Why should we believe you?" And that, of course, was Christian.

"Fine." Mary pushed the trap back impatiently and climbed through. "See for yourselves."

She knelt by the opening, and flicked each boy in

the head as he came through. Alberick was the only one who protested. "What's that for?" he asked, rubbing the back of his head. "I haven't done anything to you!" He considered for a moment. "Today."

"One on account, then," Mary said. She helped Adeline climb through, and the five of them stood close together.

The wind whistled through with a purpose, as if it had things to do and no time to waste. Mary rubbed her arms.

"Cold?" asked Zachariah.

"Of course she's cold!" said Christian. "The Bell Tower Man strikes chills into whoever is in his presence."

"But we're not in his presence," said Alberick. "And Mary's the only one who's cold."

"Of course. That means that the Bell Man has chosen the lovely Mary for his next victim! He'll probably carry her off this very night!"

Mary tried to retort but suddenly her tongue was clumsy as a drunken ox. She was flustered by Christian's use of the word "lovely." The best she could get out was a contemptuous "Hmph!"

Christian grinned wickedly at her. "Mark the way she stands, struck dumb by the presence of evil from beyond the grave!" His eyes widened and he pointed dramatically. "And what's that, over there in that corner?"

His unwilling audience jumped and turned as one body to see where he pointed. Did that corner seem darker than the others? Mary squinted. Had Christian really seen something, or was he just putting on?

No, wait...a rustling sound, and the shadows seemed to gather themselves, whispering together. The darkness rose up and up...taking form...taking the shape of – Mary's heart skipped a beat – a *man!*

The children cried out. Christian yelped in terror and jumped backwards, throwing himself off balance as he teetered near the arched opening. Mary grabbed his hand, steadied him. Then she turned and faced the shadowy shape.

As it came forward, she pushed Adeline behind her and lifted her chin in defiance. Adeline clung to her skirt and peered around her waist.

Closer yet...larger and closer...

"What – what's the meaning of this? Children, what are you doing here?"

Miss Hobbes! But it was Miss Hobbes as the children had never seen her. Hair undone. Shoes off. Dress –

"Well, bless me," Christian said.

Mary covered Adeline's eyes.

A man blustered forward, hopping as he tried to fasten his boot. His face was as red as his hair. Barent the Gatekeeper.

"What is it? I want to see!" Adeline pushed Mary's hand away from her eyes. "Oh!"

"Good heavens, we – er – I must have fallen asleep," said Miss Hobbes. She drew herself up and spoke as if she were standing in the schoolhouse, ruler in hand. "Children, you should be at your desks right now! Get away with you, and I want to hear you reciting your numbers when I mount – er – *climb* those steps to the schoolhouse!"

The children slowly descended the steps and came out into the sunshine, blinking. Mary couldn't bring herself to look at Christian, although she knew his cheeks must be as red as hers.

Adeline jumped up and down, tugging on her hand.

"What is it?" Mary asked tiredly.

"I was right! It was him!" Adeline crowed triumphantly. "Miss Hobbes *was* taken by the Bell Tower Man!"

> > < <

Sweet Inspiration

AMANDA BEAT HER HEAD AGAINST her hand. For Pete's sake, there had to be a way to make this work. The pad of paper was open, sitting on her lap, utterly and terrifyingly blank. Its white surface reflected the sun, glaring up at her. She had just under an hour now to make her deadline.

The project had been thrown at her at the last possible second: create an ad mockup for a new brand of toothpaste. "Don't rush the details," her boss had advised, "just give us a rough concept. Try to show us something we've never seen before. We need it by five o'clock."

That conversation had taken place just before lunch.

"No problem," Amanda had said gamely, while inside her heart was doing a schizophrenic dance of terror and joy. But this was her chance, this was what she'd worked for and now here it was: give us your best shot. And she would.

Lunch was out of the question, of course. She'd sat in front of the computer with her design software for the next three hours and had gotten nowhere. Finally she'd grabbed her sketch pad and made a run for the door. She had to get out of the office. These sterile walls were doing nothing for her creative juices. She needed stimulation. Motivation. Inspiration.

She'd stalked the streets for an hour, until she'd flung herself down on this stoop in frustration. Now here she sat, on some stranger's front stairs, waiting for inspiration. And as usual when she needed it, it was nowhere to be found. Oh, it would keep her up at night, smack her in the face during some movie, make her laugh out loud when she was riding the bus. But try to chase it and it would take off in the other direction.

Amanda leaned back and closed her eyes. Come on, she thought, just a little idea. Just something to get started. She pictured her ideas like a bouquet of brightly colored balloons, rising in the air, multiplying, spreading…and then she had it.

Her eyes snapped open and her hand begin to move, began to sketch, spreading shapes and colors across the page. Roughly, roughly, she cautioned herself, remembering her boss' words. Broad strokes. Don't force the details if they're not ready.

At last she dropped the pencil and flexed her fingers, working them painfully. She held the pad at arms' length and smiled. It wasn't perfect but it was a damn good start.

Amanda shoved her pencils in her purse and ran down the stairs. Her boss was right. This could be her big break, her chance to get noticed. Yes, yes, yes!

No.

She was so caught up in her happy little world that she didn't even see the tall man walking down the street toward her, holding the hand of a little girl. She ran smack into him, barely missed running over the child. Her papers and purse went flying as she stumbled backward, stunned and shaken. The man had been carrying a plastic cup full of soda and now it was all over her. She was drenched. Cold, sticky liquid was dripping down her legs. And her sketch pad – oh God, she could hardly stand to look. It was on the ground, soaked through.

"Oh, I am so sorry," the man said, even as Amanda cried, "Damn it!"

He had some sort of duffel bag over his shoulder. He pulled out an old t-shirt and started dabbing at her uncertainly. She yanked it away and wiped her face and her arms.

Ruined, she wailed to herself. All that work, her one big chance, it was all ruined. She pictured her boss sitting at his desk, waiting for Amanda to waltz in triumphantly with a brilliant idea for selling toothpaste. And instead she'd be slinking in, wet and sticky, with a pile of mush that had once been her drawing pad.

"I'm so sorry," the man said again. "I was talking to my little girl and I wasn't watching where I was going. Are you okay?"

No, she wanted to say. *I'm not okay. I am wet and I am sticky and I am ruined. And it's all your fault.*

But instead she looked up, into his wide brown eyes, and she heard herself saying, "I'm fine."

He smiled at her, and she felt herself flush. Her eyes automatically took in the fact that he wasn't wearing a wedding ring. "It's my weekend with my daughter," he said helpfully. "Her mom has her during the week."

"Oh," Amanda said, suddenly feeling shy. To distract herself, she looked down at the man's daughter, a curly-haired angel in a yellow dress holding an ice cream cone. The girl took a lick of her ice cream and smiled. Instantly Amanda's anger evaporated, and she thought, *Some things are too sweet for even the strongest toothpaste to handle.*

She laughed out loud. That was it! Forget the idea she'd had earlier, the one that was now mushy and sopping on the pavement, and just picture a little girl with an ice cream cone and an angelic smile. "Some things are too sweet for even the strongest toothpaste to handle. But for everything else, there's Ultra-White." Oh yeah, baby, that was it!

And if she ran all the way, she could still make it to the boss's office by five.

She bent down to scoop up her ruined pad and purse. As she straightened up, she gave the girl an impulsive kiss on the cheek. "You're my new favorite person," she whispered brightly.

"I've got to go," she said. "I have a meeting. It could be the most important one of my entire career."

"Oh no, and I just dumped a Coke on you!" The

man's face was full of despair, but it was also cute. Definitely cute.

"Don't worry, it was the nicest thing anyone's ever done for me," Amanda said. She pulled a damp, wrinkled card from her purse and shoved it at him. "Give me a call sometime. If everything goes the way I hope it will, I think I should take you out for a nice expensive dinner!" She laughed again as she looked down at the little girl. "Both of you!"

www.ingramcontent.com/pod-product-compliance
Lightning Source LLC
Chambersburg PA
CBHW020619150626
46552CB00025B/1547